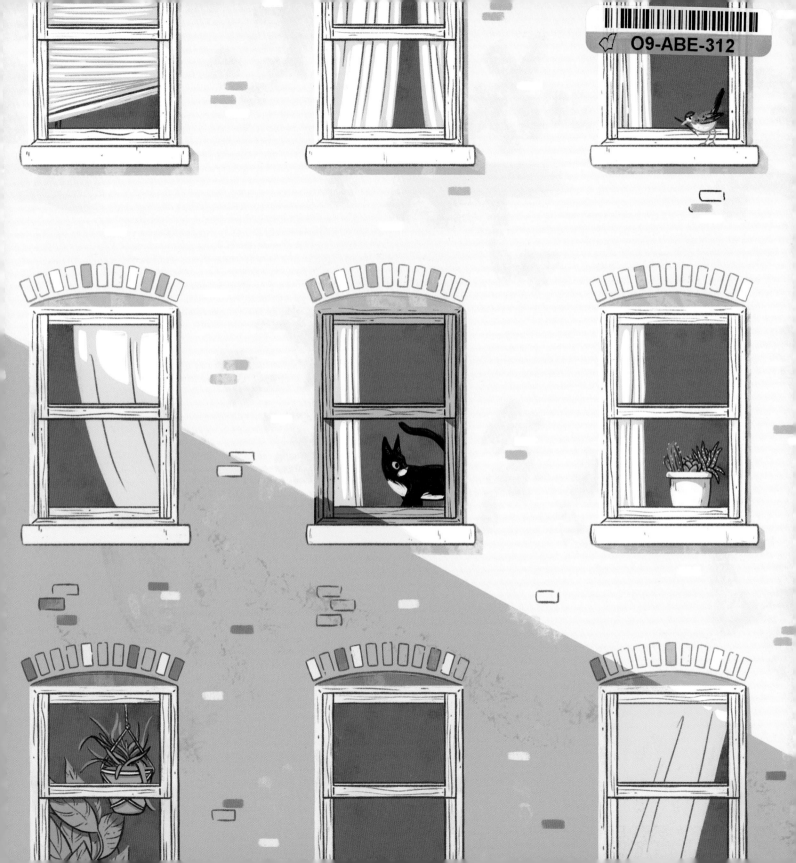

While Caroline spent many years in beautiful Colorado, I always knew at heart she was a city girl through and through. Another thing I always knew about Caroline was that she could make anything, large or small, boring or mundane, into something touching and sincere. In this book, her love of whimsy and her love of the city come together, and I hope you can find as much joy and love within the city streets as she always did.

—Alec Stutson, Caroline's Grandson and Writing Apprentice

For Jamie.

—Celia

SLEEPING BEAR PRESS™
2395 South Huron Parkway, Suite 200
Ann Arbor, MI 48104
www.sleepingbearpress.com

Printed and bound in the United States.

10 9 8 7 6 5 4 3

Library of Congress Cataloging-in-Publication Data

Names: Stutson, Caroline, author. | Krampien, Celia, 1988- illustrator.
Title: My family four floors up / written by Caroline Stutson ;
illustrated by Celia Krampien.
Description: Ann Arbor, MI : Sleeping Bear Press, [2018] | Summary:
Illustrations and rhyming text follow a young girl and her father as they
share a busy day at the park before returning to their fourth-floor apartment.
Identifiers: LCCN 2017029794 | ISBN 9781585369911
Subjects: | CYAC: Stories in rhyme. | Fathers and daughters—Fiction. |
Parks—Fiction. | City and town life—Fiction.
Classification: LCC PZ8.3.S925 My 2018 | DDC [E]—dc23
LC record available at https://lccn.loc.gov/2017029794

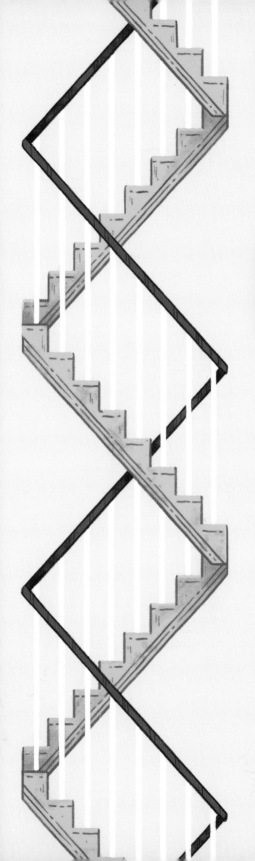
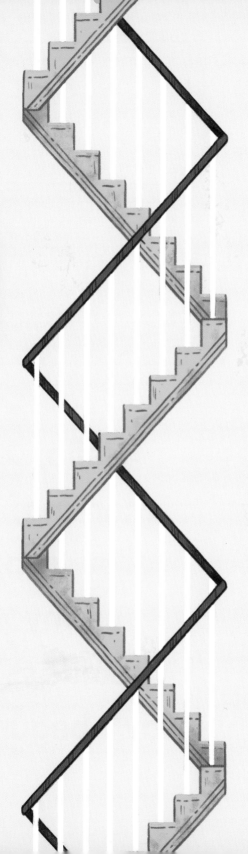

My Family
FOUR FLOORS UP

Written
by
Caroline
Stutson
and
Illustrated
by
Celia
Krampien

Hello,
morning,
yellow sun,
yummy
breakfast.
Day's begun.

Hurry, scurry, small brown pup! Goodbye, red door, four floors up.

Hello,
sidewalk,
many feet!
Goodbye,
black cat,
city street.

Hello,
green park,
bright blue
sky,
swing,
swing,
swinging
way up
high!

Goodbye,
ducklings
wobbling by.
Hello,
sand cake,
pebble pie.

Gray clouds
hover.
All complain,
drip,
drip,
dripping
in the
rain.

Goodbye, playground! Hurry, pup, climb, climb, climbing four floors up.

Hello, bubbles,
rub-a-dub,
splash,
splash,
splashing
in the tub.

Goodbye,
supper,
every bite.
One more
story,
snuggled
tight!

Hello, pillow,
warm, soft
bed,
white moon
shining
overhead.

Three friends
settle,
drift to sleep,
count,
count,
counting
pink cloud
sheep.

Curtains
billow.
Windows
light.
Goodbye,
daytime.
Hello, night.